AND THE PUPPY SURPRISE

BY
V.T. BIDANIA

ILLUSTRATED BY
EVELT YANAIT

PIC

For Justyn –VTB

Published by Picture Window Books,
an imprint of Capstone.
1710 Roe Crest Drive
North Mankato, Minnesota 56003
capstonepub.com

Library of Congress Cataloging-in-Publication Data
Names: Bidania, V. T., author. | Yanait, Evelt, illustrator.
Title: Astrid and Apollo and the puppy surprise / by V.T. Bidania ; illustrated by Evelt Yanait.
Description: North Mankato, Minnesota : Picture Window Books, [2021] | Series: Astrid and Apollo | Audience: Ages 6-8. | Audience: Grades K-1.|
Summary: Astrid and Apollo each have a special, surprise birthday gift planned for the other, and Astrid thinks she has guessed what Apollo is giving her, but as she puts more clues together, she realizes she is in the middle of a birthday mystery. Includes facts about the Hmong.
Identifiers: LCCN 2021002447 (print) | LCCN 2021002448 (ebook) |
ISBN 9781515882084 (hardcover) | ISBN 9781515883166 (paperback) |
ISBN 9781515891758 (ebook pdf)
Subjects: CYAC: Twins—Fiction. | Brothers and sisters—Fiction. | Birthdays—Fiction. | Dogs—Fiction. | Hmong Americans—Fiction.
Classification: LCC PZ7.1.B5333 Ar 2021 (print) | LCC PZ7.1.B5333 (ebook) | DDC [E]—dc23
LC record available at https://lccn.loc.gov/2021002447
LC ebook record available at https://lccn.loc.gov/2021002448

Designer: Kay Fraser

Image Credits: Capstone/Dara Lashia Lee, 61; Shutterstock: Ingo Menhard, 60, Yangxiong (pattern), 5 and throughout

Printed and bound in the USA. 4270

Table of Contents

MEET ASTRID & APOLLO

Hi, I'm Astrid. My twin brother is Apollo, and we were born in Minnesota. We live here with our mom, dad, and little sister, Eliana.

ASTRID GAO NOU

Hi, I'm Apollo! Our mom and dad were both born in Laos. They came to the United States when they were very young and grew up here.

APOLLO NOU KOU

MOM, DAD, AND ELIANA GAO CHEE

HMONG WORDS

gao (GOW)—girl; it is often placed in front of a girl's name. Hmong spelling: *nkauj*

Gao Chee (GOW chee)—shiny girl. Hmong spelling: *Nkauj Ci*

Gao Hlee (GOW lee)—moon girl. Hmong spelling: *Nkauj Hlis*

Gao Nou (GOW new)—sun girl. Hmong spelling: *Nkauj Hnub*

Hmong (MONG)—a group of people who came to the U.S. from Laos. Many Hmong from Laos now live in Minnesota. Hmong spelling: *Hmoob*

Nou Kou (NEW koo)—star. Hmong spelling: *Hnub Qub*

tou (TOO)—boy or son; it is often placed in front of a boy's name. Hmong spelling: *tub*

CHAPTER 1

Sea Blue

Astrid looked at the crayons. She tapped her chin. She did not know which color to pick. But she knew Apollo liked blue.

She read the names of the crayon colors. There were so many blues. "Baby blue, navy blue, sea blue. Eliana, what's the best blue for Apollo's shirt? Sea blue?" she asked.

Eliana was sitting in her high chair drinking juice from her sippy cup. She said loudly, "SEE BOO!"

Astrid put her finger to her lips. "Shhh! We don't want Apollo to hear!"

Eliana copied her big sister. She put her finger to her lips too and said, "Shhh!"

"You are so silly!" Astrid laughed and picked up the sea blue crayon. "Let me test this," she said.

She drew the shape of a T-shirt. She colored it in with the crayon.

"Sea blue is perfect!" she said. "Now I need to draw a funny cat."

"CAT!" said Eliana.

"Be quiet, Eliana! You are going to ruin my surprise," Astrid whispered.

"Suh-pies!" said Eliana.

"What surprise?" Mom asked as she walked into the kitchen. She was carrying a small pack of paper.

Astrid stood up. "Mom, did you get the transfer paper?" she asked softly.

Mom handed it to Astrid. She said quietly, "Yes, this is for you!"

"Thank you!" whispered Astrid. She opened the pack. Inside were thin pieces of paper. "When I finish my drawing, I can print it on this!"

Mom nodded. "Yes, we'll scan your drawing into the computer and print it on the transfer paper. Then we'll iron that onto a T-shirt."

"Will you help me iron it, please?" Astrid asked.

"Of course," Mom said. "A T-shirt will be a very nice birthday present for Apollo."

"Thanks, Mom!" Astrid said happily.

Every year on their birthday, Astrid and Apollo surprised each other with fun presents. This year Astrid wanted to make the present herself.

Apollo always said he wasn't sure whether he wanted a pet cat. But he sure liked to wear cat T-shirts! So when her cousin Lily told her about the transfer paper, Astrid knew what to do. She would draw a funny cat and put it on a T-shirt for Apollo!

"What color shirt do you want to give him?" Mom asked.

Astrid showed Mom the crayon. "Eliana and I picked sea blue."

"That's a nice color. I'll try to find a shirt to match at the store," said Mom.

Apollo walked into the room. "Find what at the store?" he asked.

"Nothing!" said Astrid. She hid the transfer paper behind her back.

"Nothing!" Mom repeated. She picked up Eliana from the high chair.

"Nuh-ding!" Eliana screamed.

Apollo covered his ears and said, "Sorry I asked!"

CHAPTER 2

Bright Moon

After dinner, Astrid saw Mom, Dad, and Apollo in the living room. Astrid could hear them whispering.

Astrid smiled. Were they talking about *her* birthday present? What was Apollo planning?

They did not see her, so Astrid snuck up to hear better. She heard the words "green" and "pink." Then she heard the word "puppy."

Astrid gasped.

Apollo turned around.

Astrid ran down the hall and up the stairs. She hurried to her room, which she shared with Eliana. She quietly closed the door in case Eliana was sleeping.

Green and pink? Puppy?

Had Apollo guessed that Astrid was making him a cat shirt? Maybe he wanted to make Astrid a dog shirt! Maybe he was deciding between a green or pink shirt.

That had to be it. Apollo knew how much Astrid liked dogs. *How funny!* Astrid thought. They would give each other T-shirts!

Astrid was sure that Apollo would draw a Teddy Bear dog. Teddy Bear dogs were her favorite in the whole world. She had read a lot about them. They were small, sweet, and soft as teddy bears. They liked to snuggle. They did not bite. They loved their owners.

She wanted a Teddy Bear dog so much. That's why she had lots of things with Teddy Bear puppies on them.

There was a knock on her door.

"Astrid?" Mom said softly.

"Come in," whispered Astrid.

Mom walked in.

"I'm checking on Eliana. Is she asleep?" Mom asked.

They both looked at Eliana's crib.

"She looks asleep to me," said Astrid.

She really wanted to ask Mom about the puppy shirt, but she knew it was supposed to be a surprise. So she said, "I'm working on my cat drawing for Apollo."

“That’s great! Show me when you’re done,” Mom said. Then she left the room.

Astrid sat down at her desk. She took out paper and crayons. Outside the window, she saw the moon. It was a perfect, white circle. It looked so bright. It made her feel happy.

The white color made her think of a cat too. Astrid started to draw a cat fishing. Then she drew a cat playing soccer. She laughed as she drew. The cats looked funny!

"Cat!" said Eliana.

Astrid jumped. "Eliana! I thought you were asleep."

She walked over to Eliana's crib. Eliana was standing up, holding her blanket.

"You need to go back to sleep. Hurry, before Mom hears you're awake," said Astrid.

Eliana sat down and pointed to Astrid's drawing. "Cat!" she said again.

"Shhh!" said Astrid.

"Did someone say *cat*?" Apollo's voice came from the open doorway.

Astrid hurried to her desk. She turned over the drawing. "No. Go away!" she said.

"Why? That's not nice," Apollo said.

"Sorry, Apollo. I mean, see you later!" Astrid said.

"Later!" Eliana echoed.

Apollo pretended to cry.

"Boo-hoo. Bye!" he said.

* * *

The next day was the day before the twins' birthday. Astrid went with Dad and Eliana to the grocery store. When they came home, she saw Apollo and Mom in the dining room.

Mom was talking on the phone, looking at her computer. Apollo stood behind her. He was smiling. Then he saw Astrid, and he poked Mom's shoulder. Mom closed the computer.

"What are you doing here?" Apollo asked Astrid.

"I live here!" Astrid said.

"Let's put the groceries away," said Dad.

"Away!" Eliana said.

Apollo pointed to the kitchen. "Go!"

Astrid frowned. She followed Dad and Eliana to the kitchen.

At lunchtime, Mom got three phone calls. Each time she picked it up, she would go to a different room. Apollo kept following her.

"What are they doing?" Astrid asked Dad.

He shrugged. "You need more rice?" he asked Eliana.

Eliana was eating a bowl of rice with water. She shrugged too.

"Who keeps calling? Why do they have to leave the room?" Astrid asked.

Dad shrugged again. So did Eliana.

When Apollo and Mom came back, Astrid asked, "Who called?"

But no one answered her.

"Please pass the fish sauce," Apollo said instead.

"Who wants another bowl of pork and green vegetable soup?" Mom asked.

"You need more rice?" Dad asked Eliana again, even though she was done eating.

* * *

Later, Astrid and Eliana were sitting on the carpet. They were working on a big puzzle. It was a map of Laos.

Apollo came and sat down next to them.

"You still like Teddy Bear dogs?" he asked. He was grinning.

Astrid tried not to smile back. She did not want Apollo to know she knew about the puppy shirt.

"Teddy Bear dogs will always be my favorite," she said.

Apollo handed Eliana a corner puzzle piece.

"Why do you like them again?" he asked.

"They are the sweetest dogs!" Astrid said. "They are tiny. They are loyal. They are the best little dogs ever!"

"Okay. Do you like green? Or pink?" he asked.

Astrid was right! Apollo *was* making her a T-shirt. He would draw a cute little Teddy Bear puppy on it.

"I like both colors," said Astrid with a smile.

Apollo nodded and stood up.

CHAPTER 3

Tae Kwon Do Cat

"Mom, I finished the drawing!" Astrid said.

For Apollo's shirt, she had drawn a cat doing tae kwon do. The twins loved tae kwon do. She used the brightest crayons. She made the cat happy and funny, just like Apollo.

Astrid showed it to Mom. "Do you like it?" she asked.

Mom held up the drawing. "This is amazing! Great job, Astrid! Let's scan it," she said.

After they scanned it into the computer, Astrid gave Mom the transfer paper. Mom placed it in the color printer. Then she printed out the drawing.

"It looks nice!" Astrid said.

Mom handed her scissors. "You can cut it, and we'll iron it onto the shirt. Cut close to the outline of the cat. I'll get the iron ready," she said.

Astrid cut out the drawing. She wished she could ask Mom about the puppy T-shirt. She wondered how Apollo drew the puppy. Walking? Playing? Maybe doing tae kwon do!

Mom said, "Here's the T-shirt. I tried to match it to the crayon color you picked."

Astrid looked at the shirt in the bag. "The color looks just like the sea! A bright blue sea on a sunny day. My tae kwon do cat will look great on it!" she said.

As Astrid gave the bag back to Mom, a green bow fell out. It landed by her feet.

Astrid bent down to pick it up. "What's this?"

Mom quickly took the bow from her. "Are you ready to iron?" she asked.

Astrid tried to hide her smile. Maybe the bow would go on her present, the puppy shirt!

Mom ironed the cat drawing onto the blue T-shirt. Astrid could see the colors showing through the paper. She was so excited.

When Mom was done ironing, she peeled the transfer paper away.

Astrid covered her cheeks with her hands. "That's so cool!" she said.

The tae kwon do cat was in the center of the shirt. The funny cat had one leg up in a high kick.

"It looks wonderful. Your brother will love it!" Mom said.

"I hope so!" said Astrid.

Suddenly, Apollo ran into the room. "Mom!" he said.

Astrid quickly tossed the T-shirt into the closet.

"What's wrong?" Mom asked.

Apollo looked at Astrid. He pulled Mom's arm, and they left the room.

Astrid heard him say, "They're all gone! There's no more left!" As they walked away, Astrid wondered if Apollo was talking about the T-shirts.

* * *

For the rest of day, Apollo seemed upset. He walked back and forth all over the house. He was worried about something. Astrid felt sorry for him.

"You want to play soccer?" she asked.

He shook his head.

"What about checkers? Or chess?" she asked.

"Not right now," he said.

"Want to help Eliana and me finish our puzzle? We have the bottom half of the country done," she said.

"Maybe later," said Apollo.

"What happened?" she asked.

"Nothing, Astrid. Everything's fine," he said.

But Astrid knew something was wrong. Apollo was usually not that quiet.

She wanted to ask Mom and Dad, but they were busy making phone calls. She did not know who they were calling.

In the evening, Astrid walked past Apollo's room. He was sitting on his bed. She really wanted to cheer him up.

"Tomorrow's our birthday. I made you a present!" she said.

Apollo looked up. "Thanks. I tried to get you something you wanted. But people bought them all. I'm sorry."

"What? What do you mean?" asked Astrid. She wondered if someone had bought all the T-shirts. Was that why Apollo was so sad? Astrid felt confused.

All of a sudden, Dad said, "Apollo, come here!"

Apollo dashed out of his room.

"What is it, Dad?" asked Astrid.

"Don't worry, Astrid. You should get ready for bed soon. Tomorrow we may be going somewhere early," he said.

"But it's our birthday tomorrow. What about our special birthday breakfast?" Astrid asked.

Dad didn't hear her. He and Apollo were walking down the stairs. Astrid heard Dad say, "We'll try something else."

Astrid went to her room. She looked at the moon shining in her window. It was so bright and white. It made her feel better, even though she still felt bad for Apollo.

CHAPTER 4

Where Are We Going?

Astrid woke up to Eliana jumping on her bed.

"Way cup! Way cup! WAY CUP!!!" she said. She jumped one more time and fell on top of Astrid.

Astrid laughed and hugged Eliana so she wouldn't fall off the bed. As Eliana wiggled in her arms, Astrid saw Mom, Dad, and Apollo standing above her.

"Happy birthday!" they all said.

Astrid sat up. “Thanks. Happy birthday to you too, Apollo!”

Apollo looked happier this morning. He was smiling a big smile. “Thanks! Now get up!” he said.

"We need to go now," said Dad.

Mom picked up Eliana. "Get dressed. We'll see you in the car," she said.

"Where are we going?" asked Astrid.

"You'll see," said Apollo.

* * *

Usually on their birthday, Mom and Dad cooked a big breakfast for Astrid and Apollo. At lunchtime they would eat another nice meal with a coconut pandan birthday cake.

Astrid couldn't wait to eat the sweet cake made from the pandan plant! But when she got downstairs, there was nothing on the dining room table.

Astrid heard the car horn *beep!* from the garage.

Apollo ran inside and said, "Hurry, Astrid!"

"Why aren't we having our birthday breakfast?" Astrid asked.

Apollo took her arm. "Come on!" he said.

In the car, Astrid tried to guess where they were going. "Are we having brunch at the Chinese buffet?" she asked.

"Nope," said Apollo.

"The sushi buffet?" she asked.

Apollo shook his head. "It's too early for that."

"A pancake place? Waffles? Wait, is it fast food?" guessed Astrid.

"No, no, and no." Apollo laughed.

"NO!" repeated Eliana.

"Please stop, Eliana. It's too early for screaming," said Mom.

Eliana crossed her arms over her chest.

Dad laughed.

"Can you please give me a hint?" said Astrid. *Are we going to a T-shirt store?* she wondered.

Apollo grinned. "We'll get your present there."

"Oh, I left your present at home," Astrid said.

"We brought it," Dad said from the front seat. He held up a gift bag.

"Thanks, Dad!" said Astrid.

"I'll open it later," Apollo said.

"So, are we going shopping?" asked Astrid.

Apollo sat back in his seat and smiled. "Kind of," he said. "But your present should be ready when we get there."

"This was all Apollo's idea," said Dad.

Mom looked back at them. "Apollo worked hard to make it happen."

"You and Dad helped," said Apollo.

Astrid did not understand. She knew Apollo was good at drawing. He could have drawn lots of puppies. Why did he need Mom and Dad to help? Mom had helped Astrid iron her drawing onto the shirt, but that was all she had helped with.

"I thought someone bought all the shirts," Astrid said.

Apollo looked at her. "What shirts?"

Astrid covered her mouth. She did not want to ruin her surprise for him. "Forget it!" she said.

As they drove onto the highway, Astrid's stomach growled. She was getting hungry.

"Wherever we're going, I hope there's food!" said Astrid.

Apollo smiled. "I think they have food, but not something *you* could eat."

"Oh no! Is it bitter melon soup?" Astrid did not like that soup. Her parents and Apollo loved it, but Astrid thought it was too bitter!

Apollo didn't have a chance to answer because Mom said, "There it is! Up ahead."

Astrid looked out the window. She did not know where they were. She saw a big brown building down the block. Some cars were in the parking lot. People were walking into the building.

"It just opened," Mom said. She turned into the lot and parked.

As they got out of the car, Astrid asked, "Where are we?"

"Follow your brother," Dad said.

Apollo led the way. Dad, Mom, and Eliana followed him. Astrid shrugged and followed too. She saw a sign and was just about to read it when Apollo blocked her view.

"No reading!" he said.

Apollo opened the big doors. They walked into a small lobby. Astrid saw a tall desk and a man and a woman standing behind it. Next to the desk was a small store. It looked like a pet supply store.

Astrid looked around. Another set of doors near them opened, and more workers came out. Astrid smelled a strong smell. Was it . . . animals?

She looked at the glass windows of the doors and saw birds in cages. Inside were more cages with rabbits and cats.

"What are we buying here? Do they even sell T-shirts?" she asked.

Apollo laughed. "Astrid, why do you keep talking about shirts?"

"Oh, *you're* Astrid!" said the woman behind the desk. "You're here! She's almost ready for you."

The woman walked through the set of doors.

"*Who's* ready for me?" asked Astrid, but no one answered. She suddenly felt nervous.

The man came out from behind the desk. He smiled and pointed to some chairs nearby. "Why don't you have a seat over here, Astrid?"

He looked at Mom and Dad. "We'll have some papers for you to sign. We have a bag of food for you to take too."

Astrid stared at them. "What is happening?" she asked Apollo.

Apollo grinned at her.

"Have you decided on a name yet?" the man asked Astrid.

"Name?" Astrid asked.

Her heart started to beat faster. Was she getting something better than a T-shirt? She didn't want to get too excited in case she was wrong.

"It's a surprise," Apollo said.

The man laughed. "That's right! Have a seat. I'm sure you'll think of something once you see her," he said.

Astrid slowly sat down. "What is he talking about?" she whispered.

Mom and Dad sat next to her. Eliana sat on Dad's lap. Apollo stood near her.

Then the doors opened again, and the woman walked out. She came straight toward Astrid. She was holding something in her arms. Something with a green bow.

Astrid could not believe what she saw!

CHAPTER 5

Loona Loona

It was *not* a T-shirt. The woman handed Astrid a small white dog!

The dog had a light gray patch down her back. The tips of her ears were a cream color. She had a black nose and big, black eyes.

Astrid held the dog in her lap. She felt soft and warm. Her ears wiggled. Her fluffy tail wagged.

"Happy birthday!" Apollo said.

Astrid could not talk.

"This is your surprise!" said Apollo.

"She's really for me?" Astrid's voice was shaking. She hoped she wouldn't cry.

Apollo nodded.

The dog stuck out her tongue and licked Astrid's hand. Astrid laughed. "It tickles!"

"We know you've wanted a puppy for a long time now," Dad said.

"Puppy!" echoed Eliana.

"We feel you and Apollo are now ready for a pet," Mom said.

"You wanted a Teddy Bear, but we got you this one," Apollo said.

"She's a Maltese mix," said the woman. "The shape of her ears makes us think she could be part Yorkie. We call those Morkies."

Astrid slowly petted the dog's head. "I don't care what she is. I love her!" she said.

The dog snuggled up to Astrid's face. She was just as soft as Astrid thought a puppy could be. Astrid was so happy.

"Thank you, Mom and Dad. Thank you, Apollo! This is the best birthday present! I love this puppy!" said Astrid.

"Well, she's five years old," said the man. "So she's not a puppy anymore."

"She's so small. She looks like a puppy," said Astrid.

"Yes, Morkies are little dogs," said the woman. "She's only five pounds, and this is as big as she'll get. The good thing is, she's an adult, so she's already house-trained."

"That means potty-trained," said Apollo.

"Potty!" repeated Eliana.

"That's very good." Dad looked at Mom and smiled.

Astrid carefully scratched the dog's chin. The dog rested her head on Astrid's other hand.

Eliana reached out to pet her too.

Soon the whole family was petting her.

"She looks smaller than in her picture on the website," said Apollo.

The woman nodded. "It's good you called when you did. The little ones get adopted right away. Many people asked about her already. And we just opened!" she said.

"We got lucky!" said Apollo. "Astrid, we were trying to get you a Teddy Bear dog. We found a breeder. But then they sold the whole litter of puppies before we could get one."

"It's not easy to find Teddy Bear dogs," said Dad.

"We looked at many places," Mom said. "Last night we checked this shelter and saw her."

"She's perfect!" said Astrid.

"Anyway, it's good to adopt," Dad said.

"It's true. Many dogs need homes," said the man.

The woman handed Astrid a pink collar. "I heard you like pink," she said. "Once you decide on a name, let me know. We'll put it on her tag. Then you can take her home."

A name? Astrid had to think of a name for her new dog! She thought and thought. Finally she said, "What if I name her after the moon? She's bright and white like the moon."

"You could call her Luna! That means moon," said Apollo.

"Yes, Luna in English! Gao Hlee in Hmong," said Astrid.

"Sounds good to me!" Dad said and gave a thumbs-up.

Eliana put her thumb up too. "Loona Loona!"

"Now we have a sunny girl, a shiny girl, a star, and a little moon in our family," Mom said.

When they walked out to the car later, the sun was shining. Luna squinted at the sun. Astrid hugged her and smiled. She had a dog! It wasn't a Teddy Bear. But it was just as cute.

In the car, Astrid gave Apollo his present.

When he opened it, Apollo smiled and said, "A cat T-shirt! Did you draw it?"

Astrid nodded.

"Thanks!" Apollo put the T-shirt on over his other shirt. "This is a cool birthday surprise!"

"If you like that, wait until next year!" said Astrid.

Apollo looked at her. "Wait, are you getting me a cat?"

Astrid smiled and said, "I can't tell you because then it wouldn't be a surprise!"

FACTS ABOUT THE HMONG

- Hmong people first lived in southern China. Many of them moved to Southeast Asia in the 1800s. Some Hmong decided to stay in the country of Laos (pronounced *LAH-ohs*).

LAOS

- In the 1950s, the Vietnam War started in Southeast Asia. The United States joined this war. They asked the Hmong in Laos to help them. When the U.S. lost the war, Hmong people had to leave Laos.

- After 1975, many Hmong came to the U.S. as refugees. Refugees are people who escape from their country to find a new, safe place to live. Today, Minnesota is home to around 85,000 Hmong.

- Many Hmong American families enjoy outdoor activities like camping, boating, and fishing.

POPULAR HMONG FOODS

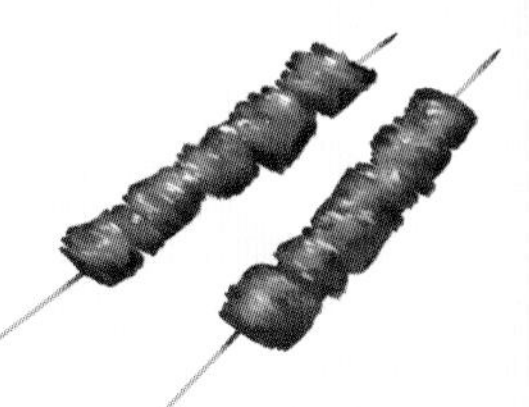

barbecued meat sticks—grilled beef, pork, chicken, or other meat on a stick

bitter melon—a vegetable that looks like a bumpy cucumber and tastes very bitter. It is often cooked in Hmong soups and other dishes.

fish sauce—a strong, salty sauce that is used as a seasoning for Hmong and other Southeast Asian dishes

mango on sticky rice—slices of mango on sticky rice flavored with coconut milk

pandan—a tropical plant used as a sweet flavoring in Southeast Asian cakes and desserts

pork and green vegetable soup—pork and leafy green vegetables boiled in a broth. This is a typical dish that Hmong families eat at mealtime.

rice in water—a bowl or plate of rice with water added to it. Many Hmong children and elderly Hmong people like to eat rice this way.

GLOSSARY

breeder (BREED-ur)—a person who raises animals to sell

buffet (buh-FAY)—a meal of several dishes where guests help themselves

loyal (LOI-uhl)—being true to something or someone

Maltese (MAWL-tees)—a type of small dog with a long white coat and a black nose

scan (SKAN)—to move a beam of light over something to copy an image

shelter (SHEL-tur)—a place that takes care of lost or stray animals

snuggle (SNUHG-uhl)—to hold close

squint (SKWINT)—to look at something through partly closed eyes

tae kwon do (tai kwon DOH)—a style of martial arts that uses kicks and punches

transfer paper (TRANS-fur PAY-pur)—a thin piece of paper that copies an image onto fabric

Yorkie (YOR-kee)—short for Yorkshire terrier, a type of small dog with long gray hair. Yorkies have tan hair on their heads and chests.

TALK ABOUT IT

1. Astrid was so happy to get a dog for her birthday. Share what you think the best birthday present would be.

2. Talk about why Astrid likes Teddy Bear dogs. What kind of dog did her family give her instead?

3. Have you ever surprised someone for their birthday? Have you been surprised for your birthday? Discuss what happened.

WRITE IT DOWN

1. Astrid drew funny pictures of cats for Apollo's T-shirt. Pretend you are making a T-shirt and draw a picture of a cat or other animal doing something funny. Write a sentence about it under the drawing.

2. Astrid's family did not want her to know about the birthday surprise. Write what they said or did each time she asked about it.

3. What was the reason Astrid named her dog after the moon? What did Mom say after they picked the name Luna, or Gao Hlee?

ABOUT THE AUTHOR

V.T. Bidania has been writing stories ever since she was five years old. She was born in Laos and grew up in St. Paul, Minnesota, right where Astrid and Apollo live! She has an MFA in creative writing from The New School and is a McKnight Writing Fellow. She lives outside of the Twin Cities and spends her free time reading all the books she can find, writing more stories, and playing with her family's sweet Morkie.

ABOUT THE ILLUSTRATOR

Evelt Yanait is a freelance children's digital artist from Barcelona, Spain, where she grew up drawing and reading wonderful illustrated books. After working as a journalist for an NGO for many years, she decided to focus on illustration, her true passion. She loves to learn, write, travel, and watch documentaries, discovering and capturing new lifestyles and stories whenever she can. She also does social work with children and youth, and she's currently earning a Social Education degree.